fiddle-i-fee

a noisy nursery rhyme by

Jakki Wood

Frances Lincoln

JAK… erhampton Polytechnic,
and … unity printshop before
setting … She has illustrated many
childr… he Animal Friends series
(wit… ooks — *Animal Parade*,
… d one enormous
… *per.*
… was selected as
… e Month.

For the Fee family – Maisie Rose and Henry

based on a traditional folksong.

First published in Great Britain in 1994 by
Frances Lincoln Limited, 4 Torriano Mews,
Torriano Avenue, London NW5 2RZ

British Library Cataloguing in Publication Data
available on request

ISBN 0-7112-0859-X hardback
ISBN 0-7112-0860-3 paperback

Printed and bound in Hong Kong

3 5 7 9 8 6 4

I had a cat, the cat pleased me,
I fed my cat by the old oak tree,
cat went fiddle-i-fee.

I had a hen, the hen pleased me,
I fed my hen by the old oak tree,
hen went chimmey-chuck,
chimmey-chuck...

cat went fiddle-i-fee.

I had a cock, the cock pleased me,
I fed my cock by the old oak tree,
cock went cockety-crow...

hen went chimmey-chuck,
chimmey-chuck,
chimmey-chuck...

cat went fiddle-i-fee.

I had a goose, the goose pleased me,
I fed my goose by the old oak tree,

goose went swishy-swashy-splishy-splashy...

cock went cockety-crow...

hen went chimmey-chuck,
chimmey-chuck...

cat went fiddle-i-fee.

I had a goat, the goat pleased me,
I fed my goat by the old oak tree,

goat went bumpity-bump ...

goose went swishy-swashy-splishy-splashy...
cock went cockety-crow...
hen went chimmey-chuck,
chimmey-chuck...
cat went fiddle-i-fee.

I had a horse, the horse pleased me,
I fed my horse by the old oak tree,
horse went ...

trit-trot ...

goat went bumpity-bump...
goose went swishy-swashy-
splishy-splashy...
cock went cockety-crow...
hen went chimmey-chuck,
chimmey-chuck...
cat went fiddle-i-fee.

I had an owl, the owl pleased me,
my owl sat up in the old oak tree,
owl went ....

tuwit

tuwoooo

horse went trit-trot...
goat went bumpity-bump...

goose went swishy-swashy-
splishy-splashy...

cock went cockety-crow...
hen went chimmey-chuck,
chimmey-chuck...

and the cat went fiddle-i-fee!

fiddle-i-fee

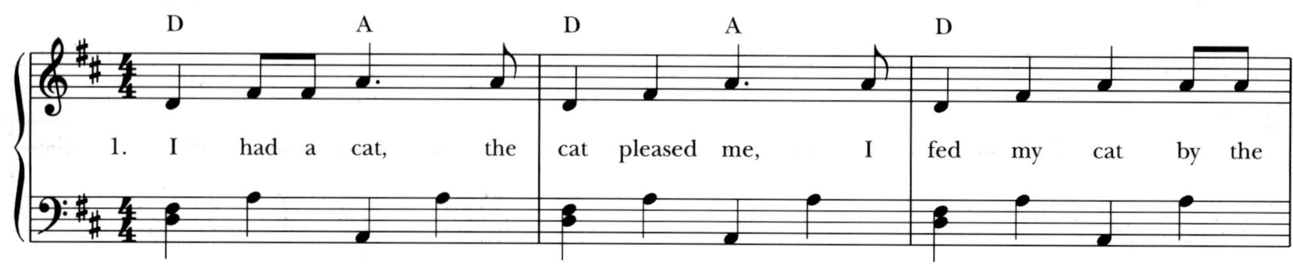

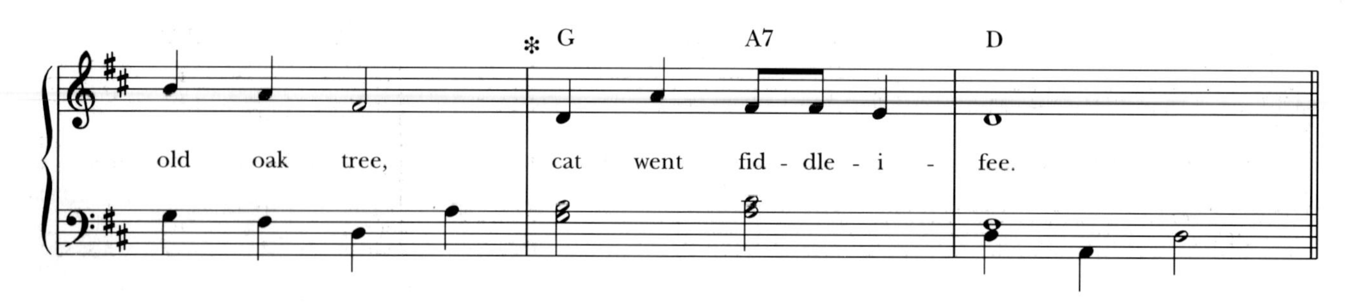

2. I had a hen, the hen pleased me,
I fed my hen by the old oak tree,
hen went chimmey-chuck, chimmey-chuck,
cat went fiddle-i-fee.

D D/A
hen went chim-mey-chuck, chim-mey-chuck,

3. I had a cock, the cock pleased me,
I fed my cock by the old oak tree,
cock went cockety-crow,
hen went chimmey-chuck, chimmey-chuck,
cat went fiddle-i-fee.

* After each new animal verse, repeat all previous noises.

4. I had a goose…

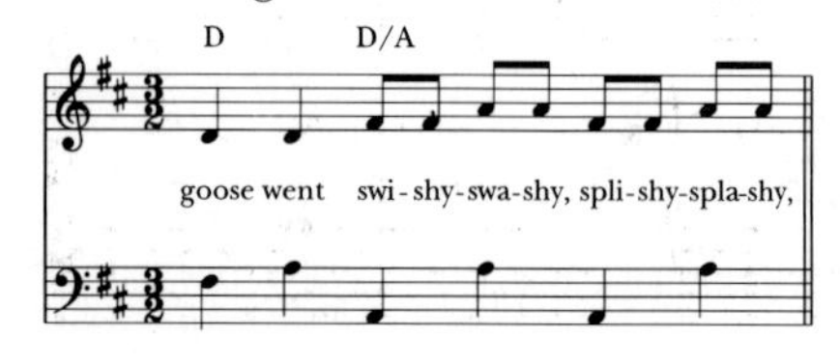

5. I had a goat…

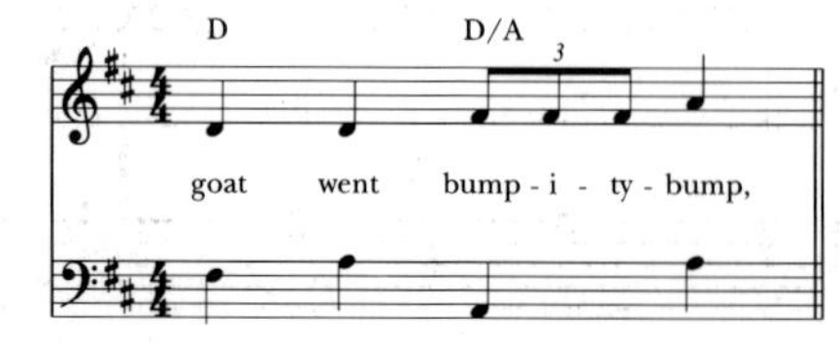

6. I had a horse…

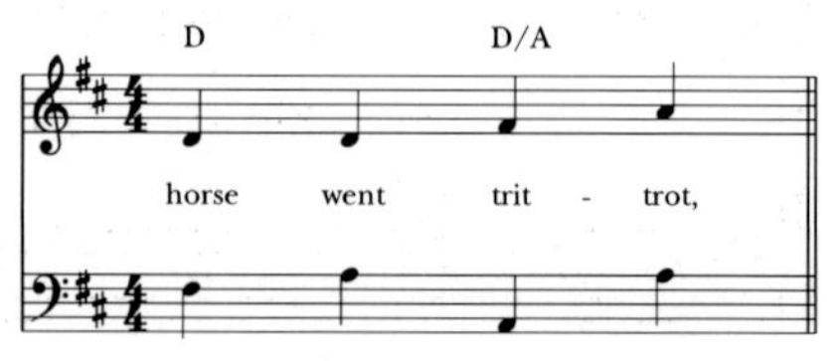

D A D A D
7. I had an owl, the owl pleased me, my owl sat up in the

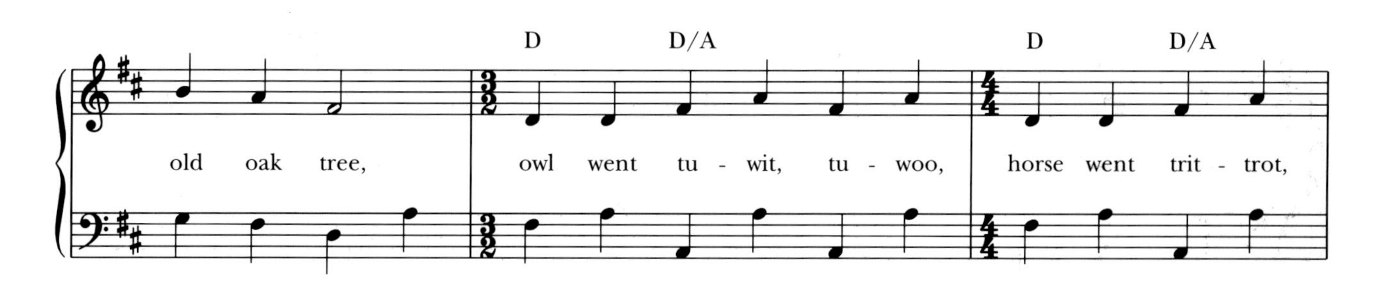
D D/A D D/A
old oak tree, owl went tu - wit, tu - woo, horse went trit - trot,

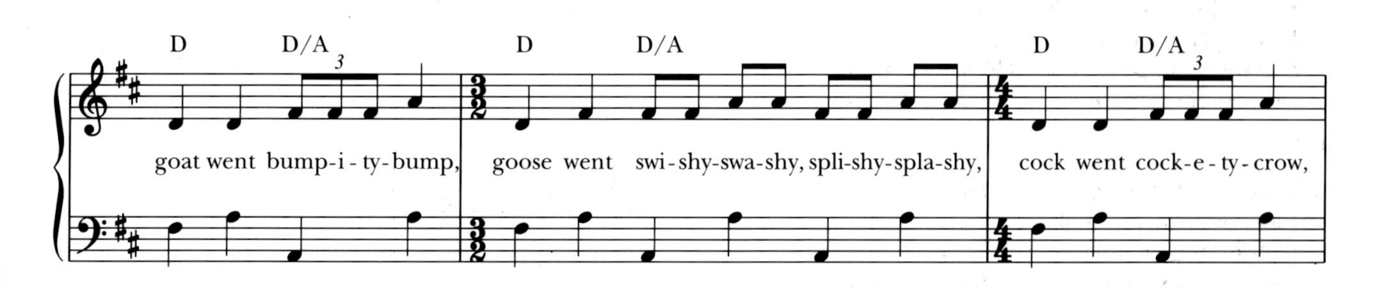
D D/A D D/A D D/A
goat went bump-i - ty-bump, goose went swi-shy-swa-shy, spli-shy-spla-shy, cock went cock-e - ty-crow,

D D/A Much slower G A7 D
hen went chim-mey-chuck, chim-mey-chuck, and the cat went fid-dle - i - fee.

OTHER JAKKI WOOD PICTURE BOOKS IN PAPERBACK FROM FRANCES LINCOLN

Jakki Wood has received high praise for her watercolours of animals: "very user-friendly, accurate, cuddly" *Books for Your Children*

ANIMAL PARADE

Featuring a nose-to-tail march-past of 95 spectacular species, from Aardvark to Zebra. Never has the ABC been such an adventure!

Suitable for National Curriculum English - Reading, Key Stage 1
Scottish Guidelines English Language - Reading, Level A

ISBN 0-7112-0777-1 £4.99

ANIMAL HULLABALOO

From dawn chorus to night-time call, more than 80 birds, beasts and reptiles raise their voices in animated uproar, with a glorious hullabaloo of sounds children will love to imitate.

Suitable for National Curriculum English - Reading, Key Stage 1
Scottish Guidelines English Language - Reading, Level A

ISBN 0-7112-0946-4 £4.99

BUMPER TO BUMPER

In the busiest, liveliest, most enormous traffic jam you've ever seen, identify and learn the names of more than 20 vehicles.

Suitable for Nursery Level

ISBN 0-7112-1031-4 £4.99

NUMBER PARADE

Jakki Wood's birds and beasts gain multiples and momentum as the score mounts to 101. Each animal has a character all of its own - and the ending will surprise everyone!

Suitable for National Curriculum English - Reading, Key Stage 1 and Mathematics at Nursery Level
Scottish Guidelines English Language - Reading, Level A; Mathematics, Level A

ISBN 0-7112-0905-7 £4.99